13 STORIES ABOUT AYANA

AMY SCHWARTZ

HOLIDAY HOUSE · NEW YORK

For Beth

Printed and bound in May 2022 at Leo Paper, Heshan, China.
The art for this book was created with gouache and pen and ink.
www.holidayhouse.com
First Edition
1 2 3 4 5 6 7 8 9 10

Library of Congress Cataloging-in-Publication data

Names: Schwartz, Amy, author, illustrator.
Title: 13 stories about Ayana / Amy Schwartz.
Other titles: Thirteen stories about Ayana
Description: First edition. | New York : Holiday House, [2022] | Audience:
Ages 4-8. | Summary: "Preschooler Ayana has thirteen adventures with her
family and her friend Harris including a jelly bean hunt, working in a community
garden, and giving her hamster, Stanley, a bath"— Provided by publisher.
Identifiers: LCCN 2021061337 | ISBN 9780823448296 (hardcover)
Subjects: CYAC: Best friends—Fiction. | Friendship—Fiction. | LCGFT: Picture books.
Classification: LCC PZ7.S406 Aac 2022 | DDC [E]—dc23
LC record available at https://lccn.loc.gov/2021061337

ISBN: 978-0-8234-4829-6 (hardcover)

one

Ayana woke up backwards.

She put her dress
on backwards

and walked into the kitchen backwards

and told her mother "Good night!" instead of
"Good morning!" and asked for spaghetti with
spaghetti sauce for breakfast instead of cereal
and milk because today was a backwards day.

two

Ayana was at the pet store. Ayana's mother was pushing a big cart. Ayana was sitting in front.

Ayana's mother put a
yellow cage with a
wheel and a water
bottle into their cart

and two big bags
of hamster food

and a book called
"How to Take Care
of Your Hamster."

Because today Ayana was buying a hamster. His name was Stanley. The pet store lady put Stanley in a little white box.

Ayana's mother carried the book home and the yellow cage and the two big bags of hamster food. And Ayana carried Stanley.

three

Ayana had a yellow Easter basket and Harris had one too.
It was Easter and Ayana and Harris were hunting for jellybeans.

Ayana found some orange jellybeans on a chair and some blue jellybeans in a dish and a pink jellybean under the spider plant.

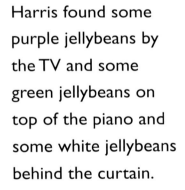

Harris found some purple jellybeans by the TV and some green jellybeans on top of the piano and some white jellybeans behind the curtain.

Ayana traded Harris a blue
jellybean for a white one

and Harris traded Ayana a green
jellybean for an orange one.

Then Ayana and Harris ate all of their jellybeans.

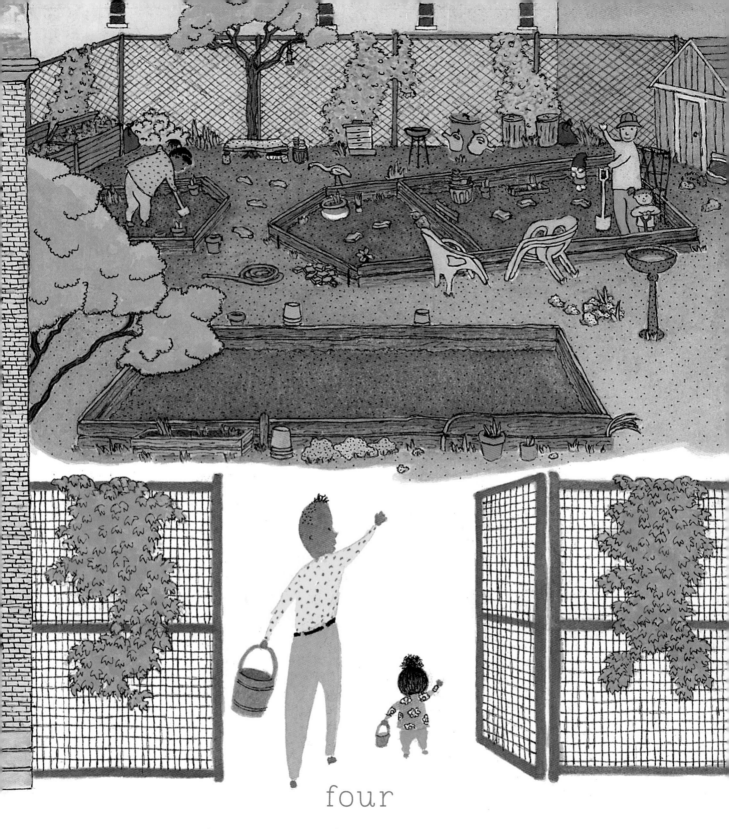

four

Ayana and Ayana's father were at the community garden.

They were planting zucchini. Ayana's father made ten little holes in the dirt with his thumb. Ayana put three zucchini seeds into each hole and covered them up with dirt.

"When will my zucchini come up?" Ayana said.

"Soon," Ayana's father said, "we'll have zucchini seedlings."

five

Ayana and Ayana's mother were on the bus. They were riding it to the end of the line. They wanted to see what was there.

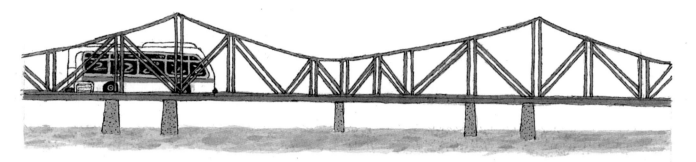

The bus went over a bridge

and up Birch Street

and down Pine.

and past a car repair shop

and another car repair shop

and another.

Then the bus stopped.

Ayana and her mother got off. There was a
chicken pot pie shop at the end of the line.

Ayana had a chicken pot pie and a glass of milk and Ayana's
mother had a chicken pot pie and a cup of tea. And then
Ayana and her mother got back on the bus and went home.

six

"**N**ext time," Ayana's mother said,
"tell me *before* you give Stanley a bath."

seven

Ayana was on vacation. Harris was watching Stanley.

Ayana slid down a water slide.

She hiked up a mountain

and back down again.

At the gift shop Ayana bought two tiny license plates.

One license plate said AYANA. It was for Ayana.
The other license plate said HARRIS because Harris
was watching Stanley and this was his souvenir.

eight

Ayana and Ayana's father were at the community garden.

They were watering the zucchini.
Ayana had a small watering can
with a pink spout

and Ayana's father had a big
watering can made of tin.

"My zucchini are almost as big as me!"
Ayana said.
"Soon," Ayana's father said, "we'll have
zucchini blossoms."

nine

The piano tuner was at Ayana's house. Ayana was starting piano lessons and her piano was out of tune.

The piano tuner played some white keys. Then he played some black ones.

Then he stood up and opened the top of the piano and reached in his hand. "What's this?" the piano tuner said to Ayana.

"A jellybean!" Ayana said.

ten

Ayana and Ayana's mother and father were in the kitchen.
They were making zucchini blossoms.

Ayana dipped the zucchini
blossoms in batter.

Ayana's father fried the
zucchini blossoms in oil

and Ayana's mother put
them on a platter.

Ayana's mother ate three zucchini blossoms
and Ayana's father ate four zucchini blossoms
and Ayana ate the rest.

eleven

Ayana and Harris were at a party. It was a block party and
it was on their block.

Ayana and Harris tossed bean bags

and went fishing

and guessed how many jellybeans were in a jar.

A giant bear made a tall animal out
of tall balloons and gave it to Harris.
It was a balloon giraffe.
"Thank you," Harris said.

Then the bear made a very little animal out of very little balloons
and gave it to Ayana. It was a balloon Stanley!
"Thank you," Ayana said.

"You're welcome," the bear said.

twelve

Ayana and Ayana's father were at the community garden. They were picking zucchini.

Ayana filled one big brown bag
with zucchini

and Ayana's father filled another.

"When can we eat my zucchini?" Ayana said.
"Soon," Ayana's father said, "we'll have lunch."

thirteen

Harris and Harris's mother and father were at Ayana's house. They had been invited over for lunch.

The mothers had lemonade and the fathers had chips and dips

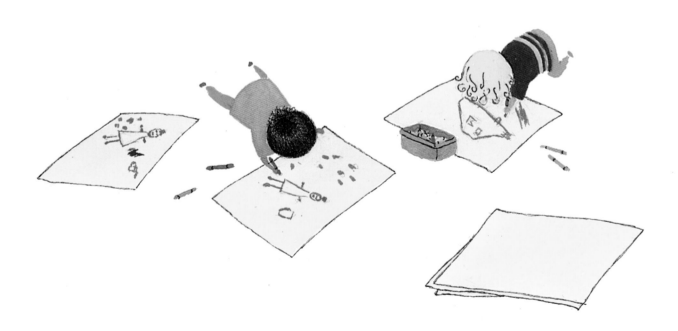

and Ayana and Harris drew pictures with Ayana's markers.

"This is me," Ayana said, "at the community garden.

This is me planting zucchini and watering zucchini
and picking zucchini."
"I like zucchini," Harris said. "What's for lunch?"

"Zucchini soup," Ayana's mother said. "And zucchini bread.
And zucchini with breadcrumbs and stuffed zucchini and
zucchini cake for dessert."